BiG HeaRT
FEELS!

by Mike and Mackenzie Morrison

illustrated by Nina Summer

Mom and Angela are at the kitchen table eating breakfast cereal.

Wow, you are a wonderful actress Angela!

Yes!
It's no fun to have
a cold. I was all
tired and yucky.

I see why he doesn't
want to play.

When they arrive at the bowling alley, they notice that her friend Alex is wearing a cast on his arm.

ALEX! WHAT HAPPENED?

Anna approaches the table, with shoes in her hands.

Here's your bowling shoes Angela!

But Angela answers: "Thanks Anna. I'm not going to need them today."

It's something my mom is teaching me. When I put myself in other people's shoes I am pretending to be them for a moment.

When I saw your broken arm, I pretended to be you. It made me feel sad because everyone would be bowling and I would be alone.

The bell rings for recess and as the kids file out, Angela notices that her friend Gina looks sad and is still seated at her desk.

Gina, are you ok?

I didn't do well on the math test. I never do well at math.

Miss Rachel puts a heart sticker on Angela's chest.

You truly have a big heart!

COPYRIGHT

Small Voice Says Press
256 S Norton Ave
Los Angeles, CA 90004
www.smallvoicesays.com

First Printed June 2020
Library of Congress Cataloging-in-Publication Data
Morrison, Ph.D, Mike; Morrison, Mackenzie
Bige Heart Feels / by Mike Morrison, P.h.D and Mackenzie Morrison ; illustrated by
Nina Summer.
p. cm.
Summary: Angela discovers how her big heart can be helpful to others.
ISBN 978-0-578-67441-4 (hardcover)
The artwork was created with color pencils, ink, gouache and digital paints.

Mike Morrison, Ph.D.

Mike's passion centers on developing leaders at all ages, from the four-year-old entering pre-school to the corporate CEO leading a global enterprise. In today's world, we all need to lead in some way and Mike has helped to illuminate that path through three books, including The Other Side of the Card.

Mackenzie Morrison

Mackenzie is a writer and artist working in the music industry in Los Angeles, CA. She currently lives in Hollywood with her two little dogs, DD & Maxine.

Nina Summer

Nina is a Swiss artist and illustrator living in Brookyln, New York. When she isn't drawing, she tries to learn how to play the ukulele. You can find more of her work at www.nina-summer.com

CPSIA information can be obtained
at www.ICGtesting.com
Printed in the USA
LVHW070434230720
661207LV00033B/403